Casey Elisha Books presents:
I Am... Short Stories

Edited by
Casey Paul
Marvin Sparks

*New diverse stories for the next generation,
by the next generation...*

CONTENTS

CONTENTS

THE I AM...
SHORT STORY
COMPETITION

The I Am... Short Story Competition launched in June 2020 for 9 – 18-year-olds with an interest in storytelling. Our aim was to encourage the creation of new diverse stories for the next generation, by the next generation.

I genuinely believe that, in order to increase representation and accurate storytelling in books, we need to raise the next generation of writers to continue the work we have started and help embed the importance of literature at an early age.

The authors of these stories took situations that reflected aspects of their realities and carved them into creative short stories.

75% of proceeds from the sale of this book will be used to purchase and distribute diverse books for free to schools, libraries and families that need them the most.

Many people are unable to get diverse books due to lack of accessibility or funds. We want to help change this.

Thank you for purchasing this book and supporting our efforts. If you would like to nominate a family, school or library to benefit from this, please email us at celishabooks@gmail.com.

A special thank you to our sponsors:

Jacaranda Books
Round Table Books
Bella and Logan Series

our judges:

Rachel Beckles
Mark Lemon
Samantha Williams
Stephen Adu-Antoh
Omar Finley

our editors:
Casey Paul
Marvin Sparks

and our competition co-ordinator, Eddie Kagutuzi.

I hope you enjoy reading these stories and find that you learn something new from the experiences of others.

- Casey Elisha

AN INNER HOPE

By Sarah Singh, 10

A few years ago, in the depths of a human body, there was an attack. The control station of the white blood cells, immune system, had sent out a signal for them to attack Liver. Apparently, it was an intruder in the body, hence the necessity to fight it. All the monocyte, lymphocyte, basophil, eosinophil and neutrophil cell warriors immediately raced towards Liver, and attacked it ferociously. After a while they left, satisfied, but poor Liver was left broken and damaged, sobbing for mercy.

Brain was in a complete state of bewilderment. What to do? Oh, what to do? She knew the news of course. One panting nerve had brought it to her, and after that she had immediately become red-eyed and worried.

"Okay, deep breaths, deep breaths," she heaved, then broke down completely. "Being in charge is such a pain! And to think I have been going on like this for months! Oh, I've not a clue what to do!"

A nerve messenger came running up to her just then, and she wiped her tears. He brought the news that a long, slender silver tunnel had been inserted into the arm and was taking in blood. That added to Brain's worries, but she felt that the tunnel was there for a good reason so told the nerve to rush and give Heart a word of encouragement to pump more blood. He obliged. Another nerve stepped up, announcing that a suspicious looking tablet, though it was quite friendly, was floating down the oesophagus, and heading straight for the immune system. Brain looked as if the world had ended at that, but she dismissed him in a voice of controlled fear: "Thanks for letting me know. You may leave now." She paced up and down her small room for a long time and then, when tiredness pounded upon her, fell into an uneasy sleep.

Nothing much happened until a few days afterwards. It just seemed like the white blood cells were doing a daily attack on Liver. Now it was red and swollen, simply crying, and crying. A little later, two nerves walked up to Brain while she was buttoning up her boots.

"Leader Brain," they acknowledged in a blunt tone and in unison, then one stepped back duly and let the other speak first. "Leader Brain," he repeated. "We have become acquainted with that suspicious looking tablet. Her name is Aza. She says she has come from the outer world to help us. Her colleagues are regularly appearing too. She tells us they are all here to convince the immune system that Liver is one of us." He bowed low, turned his back to Brain and departed without a word to his fellow nerve, being the stringy, lean, and unsociable nerve he was. The other nerve brought the news that another tablet had been spotted, named Pred. Apparently, it was a slightly worried looking doctor and was running over to tend to Liver's wounds.

***

Years passed by. Various other capsules were reported to come into the body, and soon the organs got to know them. Two of the friendliest ones were Propan, who came to encourage Heart kindly and soothe the now overtaxed Brain; and another was Siro, a cheerful and happy-go-lucky tablet, who was on the same mission as Aza.

There was now a monthly inserting-the-silver-tunnel procedure. A little crowd of organic material gathered on boats in the bloodstream to watch the blood being taken in, for this was a very popular amusement, and some got sucked in too. They went on a different adventure entirely; first, going through the shimmery tunnel, then into a large transparent tunnel with a vacuum inside, so they were sucked in and whirled round, and around and around.

Meanwhile, Brain was again controlling the body determinedly. Propan's tactful words had worked wonders on her, and she was feeling miles better. Brain had kept an eye, or rather an ear, on things by keeping a very careful track of the signals the ears sent to her. It seemed that both the body and Liver were better than ever before by what the outer people said. What a relief!

Brain heard Stomach say: "How ar' yee goin' on there, Liver?"

"Oh fine, as can be," she replied.

"Just hold on, Liver dear. You're much better now you know, and the good-hearted Siro, Aza and Pred have quite succeeded in doing what they came for, and more besides! Who knows who the white blood cells would have attacked next?" said one of the kidneys, looking daggers at where the immune system was located, for Liver was her best friend.

"Well," added one of the soft-voiced veins, "I think it's pretty lucky that it was Liver who got attacked, and not anyone else, for everyone knows that Liver is the only organ that can grow back if damaged."

"Meaning, it's a good thing Liver got attacked?" fumed Oesophagus. He was always against the veins, no matter what

11

they said. And the funny thing was, no one knew why!

"I didn't say that!" opposed the vein, getting disgusted. "I only meant that, of all the organs that could get attacked - "

"Shut up, you two!" muttered the other kidney. "There's no hope. The outer people must be thinking about transplants now."

"No! No, please!" cried Liver, dissolving again into tears and taking out her handkerchief to wipe her eyes.

"There, now ye've saddened her! Why can't ye' keep yer mouth shut?" said Stomach. The body was filled with volleys of yells and shouts immediately.

Up in the head, Brain shook her own head. She had hope of course. If there was no hope then, well, what else was there?

And sensing the hope in my brain, I smiled.

My story is inspired by my own battle with a long term chronic medical condition. I have put feelings and thoughts into the organs of my body and created a story about how they would have felt while my body was coping with the problem.

- Sarah Singh

THE CREATURE IN THE GLADE

By Alec Anderson, 11

Once there was a creature. Watching, waiting. Waiting in a glade. It had been waiting so long. Waiting for its mate to come back. It watched the sky darken, waiting for the sun to sink low over the trees and disappear from sight.

It had been waiting so long. It grunted a grunt that could have been a sigh. It rubbed its eyes with a great furry arm. It rose onto its fur-covered legs, the shaggy hair hanging off it. It stood up. Two legs. Its eyes, set beneath a heavy brow, shone dull red in the dim moonlight. It walked from the glade, into the bush. Its stride; like a man's but was also not like a man's. More like an ape. It walked gracefully despite its bulk. Another dawn, another set, another night, and still it was alone. It walked through the trees, around and around. It never carried straight on. In case the Rumblers saw it and came.

There had been animals here once. Deer, birds, fish. A complex society of animals of which he had never been a part. But now the birds had flown away. The herds were gone. The inane chatter of animal talk had ceased. Now, all was silent. He didn't care. Before, animals had all spoken at once, all the never-ending sounds of the forest. But they would fall silent when he walked past. Sometimes he caught whispered, scared voices.

"That's him!"

"He's... almost like a man."

"I've travelled, the human's call them Bigfoot" a bird's voice came from above.

He had always been an outcast. He didn't know why. He had never cared, though. He didn't care for the other creatures. Only his mate. He never paid attention to them. He knew they posed no threat to him. And he posed no threat to them. He could if he wanted, but he didn't.

The last snippet of talk he heard, before the animals all went silent, wasn't about him. He had been walking quickly through the forest. Shoulders humped, almost scared. He had been looking for his mate, a thing he didn't bother to do now, when he came out into the glade. All the animals were there, talking in hushed and serious tones. He caught snippets of conversation.

"We all must leave."

"But where?"

"Anywhere. Far from here."

A pause, then the silhouette of an owl spoke. "The humans' machines draw closer every day. More trees have vanished, with still more roads reaching deeper and deeper into the forest. Once the circle has finished, cars will soon appear. We must leave soon, or else we'll be trapped."

Then they saw him. Their eyes met for one moment. Then they were all gone, back into the forest. He never saw them again. They had deserted the wood.

Once, he had thought that something might have been coming, something huge and sinister, to the forest, and that the animals had left to escape it. It didn't matter. He could fight off any threat that came. There had been a time when he had been able to split a bear's skull, could uproot trees and roll rocks into the river with his bare hands.

But now he was old. He was now half the creature he had been, though he looked no less imposing. He no longer cared for feats of strength. All he wanted was to be left alone until his mate returned.

But he wasn't alone. The rumblers still came by. Everyday he heard them, the low growl of an engine as the pack drew closer, circling the little island of forest, before giving up and rumbling off into the distance.The creature reached a spot of flattened grass, lay down, and took refuge in sleep.

***

He woke to the sound of a bang; a loud explosion, a shot, and then a bellow, a moan. His mate. He rose and began to run. He could see, now, a light shining through the thicket of trees which marked the edge of his wooded island. If he could just get beyond it and see what was outside…

Then he stopped. He could hear voices; low voices, but shocked tones. A language he could not recognise, but understood immediately the meaning.

"Hey, Jim…" the voice echoed.

"Yeah?" a second voice appeared.

"C'mere a second."

Footsteps.

"What the - oh my..."

"What is it? It's just a bear of course!"

He could hear the sound of a body being turned over. Its limbs falling onto the cold ground.

"What the -?"

"It's a... it's him. It's really him!"

"What?"

"It's a Bigfoot."

"Oh my God."

"I'm serious. It's a female Bigfoot."

"Call the sheriff!"

"On it." A pause.

"Hey, where'd you see it?"

"It was coming out of that patch of trees in the middle of the new roundabout. I thought it was a bear and..."

The voice stopped. Then the other one spoke. "C'mon."

"What?"

"Let's go try an' find any scat or anything. We might find something the scientist guys are gonna want when the authorities arrive. Got your rifle? This could get ugly." The sound of a loud click.

"Yeah. C'mon."

And as the footsteps drew nearer, the creature slunk silently away, with its heartbeat slowing down and a tear in its eye. Back to a nest of branches and twigs, crept through into a crawl space, and sat down.

And, with the patience of a creature with nothing left to do, too weak to fight and too heartbroken to care, he began waiting in the glade once more.

I wrote this story to draw attention to environmental pressures like poaching and deforestation. I empathise with Bigfoot in the story, especially as he slowly becomes aware of his confinement.

- Alec Anderson

THE TROUBLE WITH SHOPPING

By Jemima Omole, 10

I once went on a shopping trip with my Mum, Dad and little sister. Many people are left confused when they see my family – my sister and I are black, but our parents are white. This has caused a lot of problems.

Whilst in the aisles, I saw my friend Naomi. She was getting some milk for her three-year-old twin brothers. I pulled out my phone and texted her to let her know I was there. In a flash, she replied that she was, of course – getting milk for her brothers. I giggled. The reason for our shopping trip was to get some ingredients for a cake we planned to bake later that week for a friend's birthday. We didn't have any flour, baking powder or sugar at home. Whilst Mum pushed the trolley, I dropped a new cake tin on top of our weekly shop.

After a long time of circling the aisles, I began to feel a tingling sensation at the top of my jeans – I needed the bathroom. Urgently!

I asked my Dad if I could go off to find the toilets – he nodded his head and continued to look at the rows of eggs. I hurried across to the other side of the store, suddenly reaching the toilets – they were all full! There was only one more option. I looked around to only see a smaller shop across the road. I was sure I'd be back in time and my family wouldn't even notice I had gone. I entered the quiet shop. There was no one at the till so I made my way to the loo. As I reached to open the door, three young boys blocked my way.

"What are you doing here? You dirty little moron!" one of the boys shouted. They began to pick on me because of the colour of my skin. I panicked, looked left and right and began to dodge them – I was really good at this due to my intensive rugby training. The tallest boy began to pant like he was a dog in the hot desert. Running around the store, I began to scream for help, even though I knew no one could hear me. They pushed me to the ground, and I hit my head against one of the shelves. I could feel a sharp pain in my ankle. One of the boys, stood back and gasped. There was silence. The three boys began to step backwards as they realised what they'd done – they were ashamed of themselves.

As they quickly ran away, my eyes began to close and everything went black. When I woke up and looked around I was in hospital. I didn't remember how I got there, but I saw faces with expressions I could recognise. My sister's face looked confused, whilst my Mum's looked worried. But before I registered all of that, I felt a searing pain travel swiftly up my leg.

"Ouch!" I shouted, scared and confused. "Don't worry…" a kind nurse comforted me. "You've broken your ankle, but we've set the bone, and we'll just have to put a cast on. Does that sound good to you?" I could only nod. Since I fell, I had lost track of time. I glanced at a clock near the front of the room. 6:43pm! I had fallen over around 4.30pm!

"You've been drifting in and out of consciousness for a while."

I saw the ever-calming face of my mum smiling down at me. In and out of consciousness? The nice nurse, with her strong Scottish accent spoke up again. "You can choose the colour of your cast today. We have red, pink, purple, blue, green, and yellow. You can also put on a cast cover later!"

You would think I would quickly choose my favourite colour - purple. But my friends wouldn't be able to sign it if it was a dark colour like that. I tried to answer immediately, but I couldn't speak as quickly as I thought, thanks to how weak I'd become. I tried again, more slowly. "Green, please."

After the nurse found all the things needed to apply a cast, she and the doctor got to work. First, they applied a stockinette, which was a bandage that was sort of a stocking too. Next, they put on some padding. I was happy for that, because I didn't want an itchy leg!

Finally, they began putting on the fiberglass strips after soaking them in water. Then they started to massage it. That took a while. The doctor whispered something to the nurse, and she scurried off. She came back with a small, black shoe which the doctor put on my casted foot. Then the nurse lifted my bad leg up and down. The doctor gave me a quick safety debrief, and I was free to go at last. I said thank you and rested in my hospital bed.

After a long day, I began to complain in my head about how much I couldn't do with a cast, then I looked around the ward I was in. There was a young boy in a hospital bed, his skin was pale, and his head was bald and shiny in the bright hospital light. Suddenly I realised: a cast was hardly anything in comparison to what he was going through – I was actually quite grateful for my broken ankle. I closed my eyes and mouthed a silent prayer for him and all those in need.

My story focuses on two very important topics – racism, which is very serious, and gratefulness, which is a significant virtue.

- Jemima Omole

THE CHRONICLES OF ASHLEY SMITH

By Saffron Powell, 10

Aahh I can't believe it, the most popular diva at school just asked me if I want to sit by her at lunch, of course, I said yes.

For the many of you that don't know me, my name is Ashley Smith. I am an Afro-Caribbean girl from quite a big family. I have two older brothers: one is called Dimitri, he is sixteen-years-old, and my other brother Malakhi is fourteen-years-old. Then there's me, I'm ten-years-old, the youngest in the family. Being the youngest sucks! You always get treated like a baby or you get ignored. My mom, Alisha, is a single parent. Her and my dad, Darius, separated when I was little but I still see him quite a lot.

2nd September 2019
Today is the first day of school in a new year. I am finally going to be one of the oldest children at school, but I still won't be one of the most popular. That's what every girl in my year aspires to be. School for me isn't so bad; I am quite smart, especially in English, but Math isn't exactly my strong suit. I have a best friend called Lola. We share the same birthday and we're in the same class, so we are never separated! We speak so much, one time, my teacher had to send me out of the classroom for disrupting others.

Lola was in her music class, so I agreed to sit next to Tiffany in the canteen. I have to say, I was a bit suspicious when she invited me to her table, because she calls Lola and I dorks. My fears were completely right, she embarrassed me in front of the whole school. I was just picking out my dessert (jelly, my favourite) when she called my name. "Ashley come here" she shouted. I quickly turned around to find her waving her hand at me, but disaster struck as I was walking towards her. She stuck out her leg and I fell face-first into my jelly.

It was then that I heard a familiar voice; I realised it was my crush, Tristan. I quickly stood up, horrified that he had to see me like this. "Are you alright? I think you have a little something all over your face," he asked caringly. "Yeah I know, it is probably my lunch. Thanks for telling me," I replied, wishing I could disappear into the wind. I couldn't believe how cringe I was being, despite looking like a total imbecile covered in red, sloppy jelly. At that exact moment, Lola came running in and screamed at me. "OMG I just heard what happened, are you alright?" I was planning to put on a brave front for Lola but I just couldn't help it, I burst into tears right there on the spot. That didn't help anything, because as well as having the remains of my jelly on my face, I had snot and tears. I looked like a very ugly monster.

2nd October 2019

Year 6 are going on their residential trip, and I am so excited. I have never been to France before without my parents. I am also a bit nervous because this means four days with no parents! But at least my BFF Lola will be there to laugh and joke with me when I can't get to sleep. I was just watching some TV when my mom called me to say that she is going to drop me off at school because the coach is leaving in 20 minutes. Just then, all the nerves washed over me and I realised how much I was going to miss my mom.

I gave my mom a short but loving hug and a kiss as we pulled up to the meeting point because the whole coach was watching. I promised to video call her as soon as I got to the site before rushing off to save Lola a seat next to me on the coach. When we arrived, the girls' cabin was fancier than I thought considering it was in the middle of the woods. The four days were the best days of my life; Lola and I bonded more than ever laughing and joking, I even got closer to Tristan considering we could barely talk during the activities. I also won a keychain in a rock climbing event. Who would have thought that I would be good at rock climbing?

What made the trip even better, was that Tiffany apologised for what happened in the canteen. Right there and then, I had the hard choice of choosing whether to forgive or hold a grudge. I had spoken to my mom about forgiveness many times before and she taught me that the act of forgiving is very important in life. I wanted to do the right thing and make my mom proud so I forgave her.

I guess Tiffany and I are frenemies now, (friends but still kind of enemies). We only have short conversations in the canteen and I have only sat with her once or twice but that's a start. Bye for now.

I wrote this story, which is a collection of diary entries, because it relates to my life. At school there are lots of different types of people and I wanted to share my experiences. I want every diary entry to end with a moral or affirmation. In this case 'I Am...forgiving.'

- Saffron Powell

A SUNNY DAY

By Mayomi Omogbehin, 15

Bunmi perched on the narrow, bum-numbing bench of her regular bus stop, college folder wobbling on her lap. Instead of tunnelling through the pages in front of her, her mind wandered around the fact that today was the perfect kind of day. The delicate balance of weather when the sun cast a vibrant glow on everybody's faces, eliminating the need for a selfie filter, but the light breeze prevented any sweaty discomfort.

Her mind wasn't balanced with it. This coursework had been due last week, but Mr Mart had spared her, on the condition that it be done today. As usual, she'd gambled with her time and was now racing to complete it five minutes before classes started, at a bus stop that was 20 minutes away. An engine groaned behind Bunmi. As the double-decker bus hauled itself to a stop, a figure marched past. He was slightly shorter than her, a couple of years younger and intently focused on something she couldn't see.

"Ay, Nana!" she had to jog to catch up. "Where've you been?"

They didn't go to the same school, but ever since Nana was an unusually cocky, backpack-clad year seven, and Bunmi was an attention seeking year nine, they'd been going to the same bus stop. Despite that, he barely spared a glance.

"Bunmi, hello there!" a grin darted across his face. "I've been a bit of a troglodyte for a while but I'm back now and better than ever!"

Nana jabbed her arm. He had this habit of using fancy words that Bunmi would never have heard of at his age.

"What?" Rubbing her newly bruised shoulder, she was still speed-walking in an attempt to match his pace. "The bus is behind us. Where are you going?"

Nana brandished his arms, "You're taking the bus? While the sun beckons you out here?" Bunmi rolled her eyes. Despite all the grandeur, he was right; she was already so late that taking the bus wouldn't make much difference, plus she needed to prepare herself for Mr Mart's fury.

While Nana rambled on, the sun cast its shadows. The massive oak tree that she passed every day, the one with its roots beginning to grapple their way out of the ground. The brightly coloured council bin with its limpet-like pieces of chewing gum. The bloated black bin bags straddling it. All of these familiar landmarks fronted their own darker siblings.

A thought occurred to Bunmi, "Nana, what did you mean by 'troglodyte'?"

Nana began, "Well, that depends a lot; troglodyte can have many meanings, for example on one hand -"

"I didn't ask ..."

"It can denote an idiotic caveman ideologically, but on the other hand you could be talking about a prehistoric cave dweller, you know. Isn't it scorching out here?"

Before answering, Bunmi sighed loudly. It irritated her when Nana acted like she didn't understand polysyllabic words. Even when she didn't.

"No, it's not that hot. Pretty nice, actually" she huffed. Not that Nana stopped for the answer. "It's boiling" he continued. "But better than the rain we're always plagued with. Way better than the miserable grey sky. It's a lot better than rain." He spoke as if it were a magic spell that needed repetition to come to fruition.

They reached the dusty yellow traffic island where Bunmi and Nana's paths diverged. She was glad; Nana was always talkative, but today the rambling was on a senseless level. Instead of turning left, as on a normal day, though, Nana was striding forward.

"And where are you going?" Bunmi asked, as she veered right. She knew his school was just at the end of the road and going straight simply lead to the high-street.

"There is an aim I have for this day and school is not part of that aim!" Nana shouted over his shoulder. Bunmi briefly pondered if, as a somewhat sister-like figure, she should intervene. But the thought disappeared under her homework concerns. And anticipation of Mr Mart's inevitable haranguing after he flipped a few pages of her essay. And the fact that this was her third time being late so she would be having to pay the price for that. But then her thoughts turned to the realisation that, like Nana, maybe she didn't need to turn up at all. She swivelled around and walked backward.

On the high street, the sights were the same. Aunties strolled along with phones clamped between a shoulder and an ear, colourful printed scarves wrapped around heads, and signature trollies trailing behind. Loud bartering took place at the typical markets selling plantains and yams outside while cuts of meat were butchered and drilled inside. Bunmi walked past the usual loud speakers booming highlife, heavy baselines felt in each step.

27

Then why was Nana so excitable? She was embarrassed by the way he brazenly helloed everyone who made eye contact. The mortification only increased as she was dragged to the sports store. That was when Bunmi hesitated.

"You're going into a store that's next to your school, in your school uniform, while you're bunking off. You're baiting yourself out, mate!"

"Stop worrying – you're killing the mood! But just to keep you satisfied…" Nana yanked off his blazer and tie, then dropped them onto the floor. "It was too hot anyway."

"What the…" Bunmi cursed, staring behind Nana as he ambled around the store. The last time she met him on the way to school, she didn't remember him being this irritating. Although, that last time seemed to be a grey murkiness in her mind. Then her eyes widened. She'd cracked it. She marched towards Nana, who was standing by a shelf of trainers.

"Are you on something?" Bunmi demanded.

"I like the look of these, don't you?" Nana beamed, holding up a pair of neon trainers. If she looked at them too long, Bunmi thought that they would blind her. She sucked her teeth. "Are you even listening?"

"What did you say? These would look great because I have so many dark hoodies that if I wore these with them then I would look so bright, like a light and…"

"Are you on something?"

"What? Of course not – don't be silly!" Nana guffawed. Bunmi watched his face. She hadn't noticed those black shadows under his eyes. His pupils weren't dilated, though. Bunmi continued glaring as he scampered off to the counter. If Nana was going to buy ugly trainers, that was his fault, she thought. Until she saw the price.

"No way, Nana. You can't buy these!" she hissed.

Nana frowned. "Why are you being such a killjoy?"

"You're not serious?"

His face dimmed. "Lucky for you, I'm paying, so stop bothering me – I didn't ask you to join me, so you can go away and stop being a nuisance!" he snapped.

"Fine!" Bunmi didn't look back as she walked out of the store, past the chicken shop, past her old school, and flumped onto the bus stop seat. There had always been kids in school that everybody knew took drugs. But in all her years of knowing him, Bunmi had never anticipated that Nana would be doing it.

Her eyes drifted towards an old man approaching. His white hair, bright against his dark skin, was matted. Bunmi cringed as he ambled down the street, mumbling to some foggy mirage, hoping she wouldn't be the person he chose to sit next to. She quietly sighed when he drifted further down and conducted a one-sided conversation with somebody else. She'd seen him before, and she'd seen others like him. There seemed to be one in every borough. Had she not been alone, she'd probably be laughing right now, remarking on how crazy people in London were. But there was something about this man that seemed more unwell than crazy. And was it the rambling that made him an uncanny reminder of Nana?

Thinking of Nana, he hadn't explained what he'd meant by "troglodyte". Caveman? Mr Mart had been going on about some sort of Greek cave story the other day.

"Oh, Bunmi, there you are! This is my sister, Amma. She's on her way to uni..."

Bunmi whipped around to see Nana, chatting to a girl that looked only slightly older than her. The closer they walked, the more she realised how much they looked alike.

"Hi..." said Bunmi.

"Did you know that my brother was playing truant?" asked Amma. Bunmi squirmed under her piercing glare. Before she had to answer, it shifted back to Nana. "You ok though? Not feeling dark?" she probed. "Does she know about your..."

"There's nothing to tell!"

Amma stared. She didn't look like a girl concerned about drugs. "Did you take your...?"

"I told you I feel fine now – I don't need anything!" Nana exploded. "Don't you have somewhere to be?" He turned on his heels and stormed off, the sun baring down on his back. Bunmi couldn't ignore the tall shadow trailing behind.

I've done my best to represent an environment I have grown up in, as well as experiences that many in my community may have faced but aren't addressed very much. I hope people will be able to read this story and relate to even some of the smallest details.

- Mayomi Omogbehin

REALITY

By Faye Williams, 12

Never would I have thought that it was possible to feel alone in a room filled with people.

Sorry, where are my manners: my name is Nina Rose. I have curly hair, hazel brown eyes and fair, light, brown skin. I have a sister called Trista and live with my mom and dad. I think it would be easier to start from the beginning of my dreadful week.

Monday
I am seriously thinking about skipping school for about, oh, I don't know, forever! Now don't get me wrong, I love education, but my school is different. In most high schools you socialise at play time, right? Well at my school our playtime is Tiktok, Snapchat, Whatsapp, Twitter, Instagram you name it. Sounds great, you say? Well, it's not.

Now before you think I'm grumpy just because I don't have a phone, don't. I have a phone, but what I don't have is my friends. Sure, physically my friends are here but mentally they are in a world of their own. For example: in school my friend is Mia, but online she is *BeautyQueen1* with over 1 million viewers. I would be happy for her if talking to her wasn't like talking to a dummy in a shop window; boring and pointless.

"Hey Mia, what are you up to?" I asked.

"..." she replied.

On the outside I'm a pretty calm person, but on the inside I was shaking her furiously. She pulled something out of her pocket, eyes still glued to her phone as if it could grow legs and walk off, and mumbled, "Here, you are invited to my party or whatever."

She passed me the invitation (by "passed" I mean dropped it on the desk) and headed to class like a mindless zombie. I started reading the invitation: "You have been invited to Mia's 13th birthday party. You must bring your best outfit and your phone because it's a tiktok party (you're welcome in advance). This Saturday - don't be late!!!"

Ugh!!!

Tuesday

My favourite parts of the school day are home time and class. That's when I'm not in the phone-glued, zombie, kid apocalypse. Another reason class is interesting is that we have plenty of class jokers. Laughing cheers me up. I wanted to talk to Mia about her screen time, but indirectly because telling Mia to spend less time on her phone would be like putting fish food in a fish tank and telling the fish not to eat it.

"Mia, out of all parties, why a Tik Tok one when you've had about 3 in a row?"

She looked at me as if I just asked "are we in school?"

"OMG! Nina, you don't know!?"

"Don't know what!?" I was a bit alarmed.

"Tiktok parties are the new trend!"

Sometimes I hate my life.

Wednesday

Today I was on a top secret mission assigned from me to me. I trudged to the head teacher's office, butterflies stampeding in my stomach.

Knock knock

"Come in," said Mr Chapman. "Ah Miss Rose, what a pleasant surprise. What do I owe the pleasure of your visit?" he asked cheerily.

"Well, sir, I was wondering if I may make a speech in the hall tomorrow at 2pm?" I stammered.

"And what might this speech be about?" he asked in a serious tone that just made me more nervous.

"A f-f-fight against phone addiction sir," I stuttered. He gave me a death stare that lasted what seemed like an hour, but was probably less than only a minute.

Finally, he responded. "That's an amazing idea. I don't see why not."

Never in my life had I been more happy to hear those words.

Thursday

I stepped on to the stage, my legs as weak as twigs, with sweaty palms and a chest beating faster than Usain Bolt's 9.58 100m dash, but I took a deep breath and began.

"Fellow children, it has come to my attention that phones are taking over your minds and as a result you are missing out on reality. Put your hand up if any of you have climbed a mountain. I see no hands raised. Well I bet about over 50% of you have used it as an Insta background, however that's not reality so stop going up against it. Thank you." I felt so pleased with myself.

"Yo Nina, are you done?" asked Braden, a boy in my year.

"Yes?" I said confused. Suddenly, everybody fished out their phones with a collective sigh of relief. I give up!

Friday
I am so confused because today's break time was different. Everybody was actually socialising for once. I guess my speech did have a good effect after all. To my surprise, Mia and I had the best conversation we've ever had in years! And that's not even the best part. Everyone cheered for me as they realised they were having a better time without phones and social media. I had never felt so happy in my life.

Saturday
Yesterday was amazing and very different, everyone was having fun. So why am I sitting here alone while everyone's on their phone? Well, it was fun while it lasted.

If you feel that you can make a positive difference, don't be scared even if it doesn't last. You may end up as happy as I was. Think about it.

Phones make me feel alone in a crowded room. I hope this story encourages readers to spend less time on their phones and more time with friends and family.

- Faye Williams

CHILD OF SPRING

By Scarlet Davies, 16

My heart stuttered and rapidly pounded in my chest, panicked thoughts clouded all logic. My brain screamed at me to stay inside the car: our own little pocket of warm air where results of any kind didn't matter, and I could cover my eyes to avoid the groups of students swarming around us. Besides it was safer here, and I didn't want to risk catching anything while I was around the sweaty mass of bodies, practically crawling with infections. I had enough scarring memories to be wary of any form of communication with others. But my mother firmly told me to join them. At her order, I put on my mask - still a scratchy, unfamiliar item - and meekly followed the others as we all walked towards the bitingly cold school gates one last time. Everything seemed bleaker than usual despite summer having blossomed a few weeks ago; it was almost as if the earth was grieving for the many human lives ripped away from existence.

I still remember the first time I'd ever seen this building. I was a lot more wide-eyed and optimistic, certainly not worried about the scrape of a hand against someone else's, or their warm breath on the back of my neck. Now I almost seemed paranoid, avoiding others like the plague. This year, everything was cut short: school, exams, even our last chance to say goodbye had been robbed from us. I couldn't help looking around at the faces covered with thin fabric, wondering who, if anyone, would be next. Contrasting to the first day of school, when we all clung to each other like hot glue, it almost felt like a betrayal to each other.

No longer could my classmates walk side by side, nudging and elbowing each other as they went. Everyone's worried expressions were distorted by masks of different shapes and sizes. Although, typically some people weren't wearing them correctly; it seemed that not everyone was adhering to the restrictions. Some tried in vain to stay two metres away from each other while others openly hugged and held hands. I couldn't understand how they could carelessly toss aside such rules. Didn't they know what the consequences could be?

Reaching the iron gates, I searched the crowd, practically vibrating with nervous energy, for a familiar face I could trail behind. I saw a few, but none that looked willing to put up with me for more than a few minutes. Sighing, but still riddled with anxiety, I succumbed to walking up the path alone, in silence while I listened to the others' idle chatter. Just like the current cold atmosphere of the country, the trees had already started shedding their leaves: spiralling onto the ground like scraps of crimson lace.

It was still odd to me how, despite the contagious fear of the pandemic, we were now allowed in another's company, if only for a short while. I had lived in a world of online homework and constant boredom for months. With the news constantly blaring out each statistical damnation, I'd grown scared of huge crowds or even random strangers walking alongside my house. It was like fighting for survival by stubbornly avoiding the people you cared about. But I'd learnt that lesson the hard way, and I was planning on sticking to it even if others chose to ignore the red flags.

As I neared the tables piled with cardboard envelopes at the top of the path, I noticed two of my friends milling around, waiting expectantly for someone. While I'd been trying not to, I found myself looking for the third figure that used to stand by them. Of course she wouldn't be there, I told myself, I was just being stupidly naive. But my eyes unknowingly crinkled into a smile for the first time that day as I observed the others. Louise looked the same as always: short, curly, brown hair and a loud voice echoing over the chaos, but she'd dressed up for today with a scarlet coloured top and a stylish pair of trousers. Cecilia was much the same: her dirty blonde hair was straightened at her shoulders, and she wore a denim jacket over a maroon dress. Cecilia was easily the prettiest out of us, she always had been, and tended to dress slightly too fancily for the occasion. I suddenly felt out of place in my plain shorts and band t-shirt that I'd owned for longer than I could remember.

A lump in my throat formed as I realised this would be the last time we'd all be together, and it was being spoiled by the underlying anguish we all felt. We'd gone to the same schools throughout our lives. I was confident that I could tell other people all about their childhood because it was identical to mine. I knew most of the secrets that lurked under their skin: how uncertain we'd all felt growing up, how desperate Louise had been to find a boyfriend, and how jealous she was of Cecilia who had one. I knew, despite how much I envied her appearance, Cecilia had struggled with her weight: obsessed over her looks and had often skipped meals to look thinner. I knew, even though I wanted Louise's extroverted facade, that she had been bullied at her last school and had moved to the current one to escape the torrent of teasing. I knew she tried too hard in front of others and showed off a lot because of it. And they knew how I closed myself off to people and lurked behind others when the worst possible scenario had happened a few months ago. That awful circumstance had been used to create the ropes of our relationship, binding us with our shared recollections, and by the remembrance of someone taken from us far too soon.

We immediately struck up conversation, steadfastly staying two metres apart. Cecilia happily clutched an opened envelope, but I didn't ask what she'd received straight away. I already knew she'd done better than I had. It was an unspoken rule that Cecilia (who had an enviable work ethic) accomplished more than me, and I accomplished more than Louise (who had an appalling revision schedule). Most of her teachers expected Cecilia to get high grades, especially in Art. You had to be there to experience her talent first hand; she was just born with it, and it was her calling. She will be successful too, when she continues into further education, which Louise and I silently brooded over as we struggled to figure out our own aspirations.

Nearing one of the many chipped oak tables set up outside of our towering school buildings, I stated my name in a trembling voice and was handed an identical brown envelope. Beside me, Louise stood in the middle of an anticipating group of teenagers as she enthusiastically reacted to her scores. Not wanting anyone to see my results until I'd processed them myself, I walked off into a corner and opened the sticky seal with shaky hands.

A wave of relief, with a dash of pride, washed over me. My results were even better than I'd hoped. But I hugged the envelope to my chest, thinking about how fake the little bold numbers on the page looked. We'd never taken these exams, but still, we had to live with these results for the rest of our lives. I couldn't even think of a day when the pandemic would be over and we'd be allowed to act normally again, yet here was a year of young adults going out into the broken, contaminated world with their sheets of paper, ready to face the onslaught and continue the cycle of such fragile routines. It was inspiring, how even from the ashes of so many deaths came new life.

But that didn't stop me from thinking about how someone who

should have been collecting their results with us today was no longer able to. Our little group - Louise, Cecilia and I - used to include another girl. Alice had been at our school until a few months ago, before she started violently coughing and had to be hospitalised. While the rest of us were forced to stay at home and quarantine, Alice had begun slowly fading away. As she struggled to wheeze her last breaths, I hadn't even been able to visit her for fear of catching the virus.

She died alone, void of a comforting touch or a final embrace in her stuffy room, with even hospital workers staying two metres away. I had been bitter for months about how life had turned out, and how the group of us, best friends for years, could be split up by a few germs that had passed the dreaded disease on. After the funeral, a morose affair, we all coped with Alice's death in our own separate ways; I'd thrown myself into unnecessary work, while Cecilia and Louise constantly showed off for validation, attempting to prove they were still moving forward. At the end of the day, we were all trying to live in our own way, without any of us communicating to the others that we needed help.

It was now that I thought of Alice. Looking out at all the other students looking forward to their own future. Alice would never have the pleasure of receiving her exam results, graduating or even seeing the rest of us continue into the real world. This was the end of an era; we were all going our own ways, but Alice had gone much further away than the rest of us were expecting.

And now, about to finally leave school and my friends behind, I grew nostalgic for the days when nineteen was just a year and friendship meant forever. The three of my friends had been the ones I'd spent the best moments of my life with. Looking at two of them now, all grown up, I could still remember sitting in the playground, doubling over and trying to breathe as we all gasped with laughter. There was no one else but us who would ever truly remember our experiences as our own.

Alice would live within our thoughts, because I don't think I could ever forget her. With that weighing on my mind, I walked out of the school gates for the last time ready to start a new chapter of my life. Carrying so much tangible fear and uncertainty around me these last few months, I felt stifled and claustrophobic. But in the middle of a pandemic, I'd just experienced a new wave of achievement, a glimpse of hope wedged between the horror of reality. People were going about their normal lives, and that sort of unabashed bravery while we were all struggling to cope was exactly what we needed. I noted that Alice would have been proud of the remaining three of us as we shifted from grieving to moving onward.

And together we'd slowly move forward, even if it was a few measly socially-distanced steps at a time.

The story is loosely based on my experience of going into school for the last time to collect my GCSE results, and I thought it would be a great piece of writing to give people my age and younger hope that despite the fear of the virus, not everything will end.

- Scarlet Davies

THE IMPORTANCE OF BEING BOLD

By Jasmine Omogbehin, 17

As Lolu found herself in the limp arms of what she presumed had once been a brand new salon chair, she was immediately reminded of why she would not be coming back. Enitan seemed to think that if she did a quick job blow-drying Lolu's hair, her singlehanded creation of split ends and the tufts of hair torn from Lolu's scalp on the blow-drying comb would go undetected. Lolu was sure 'Simi's Salon' down the road would treat her hair with greater grace as, despite their brow-raising prices, they retained an ardent customer base. Lolu had tried to book other hairdressers but it was as if they had all conspired to only have availability on Tuesday and Wednesday. Her job interview was tomorrow, and her own hair braiding skills left much to be desired. This rendered her returning to Enitan, a necessity, as she was the only local hairdresser willing to do Lolu's hair today at such short notice.

Despite the willingness of Enitan to schedule Lolu in at any time, neither of the two seemed to particularly value the other's conversation. The ability to construct a conversation founded on faux interest in the weather had never been Lolu's forte. Whenever Lolu attempted to feign interest in what Enitan had been up to the past week, she was met with a "nothing much" or "just hair." Lolu did not persist as she did not really divulge much of herself in discussions either. Anyway, it truly did seem that all Enitan did was work as she was constantly receiving calls from desperate clients. Therefore, the nasal babbles of the morning's news anchors were a suitable sealant for the gaps in their conversation. Today's headlining news story was about a fugitive woman going by the name of Miss Tanine.

"As she has managed to evade arrest multiple times, little is known about Miss Tanine," said the correspondent. "However, she is believed to have headed a string of scams and caused the death of local handyman, Victor Timothies, after a confrontation between the two led to her assaulting him. The police appeal to any witnesses of the incident or members of the public with further information to come forward."A poorly pixelated image of Ms Tanine appeared on the screen alongside two numbers which the public could contact regarding the case.

Lolu craned her neck to get a better view. Enitan tapped the comb against the chair impatiently. "Stop moving."

"Sorry." Lolu fixed her position.

Her stomach whimpered. If she could stay still, she supposed Enitan could finish faster, enabling her to get food faster. Lolu was just grateful for the TV; it truly made the next few hours possible to endure."It's finished." Enitan handed Lolu the oil smeared mirror. Instead of the loc-like, mid-length undulating twists Lolu had envisioned, the twists atop her head were straight with curly ends that sat dormant at her shoulders. They didn't frame her face well; simultaneously ageing and infantilising her. "Thank you! I love it!" Lolu manufactured a smile. It was not the first time Enitan had not quite got her style right. She was naive for expecting anything different. A bolder person would not have repeatedly found themselves with such a predicament; they

42

might have insisted Enitan take out the twists and redo them to their liking, but Lolu doubted Enitan could do much better. Besides, Enitan did not ask for too much monetarily. Lolu used to be glad of it too; it saved her the past embarrassment of irritating the hairdresser by attempting to negotiate on the price. This style, though not ideal, would suffice for her interview. She just needed to focus on giving a good impression. If she got the job, she would be able to afford to pay 'Simi's Salon' a visit.

Lolu departed from Enitan's apartment with her shoes half-on half-off and her stomach now roaring as the smell of chicken tikka masala curry wafted through the block's corridor. She hated walking through these narrow corridors out of fear of encountering hooded youths that lurked around the stairwell approaching girls like her, but it was preferable to entering the urine scented lifts.

Lolu sighed in anticipation as she noted a hooded figure with peeping curls in her direction. He seemed to look her up and down wordlessly, before pausing to squint curiously at her head and walking past her like a dog that had lost interest. Lolu reached for her hair self-consciously. Was it really that bad? No! She slapped her forehead realising her shoes were still undone. No wonder he looked at her like that. Lolu crouched down to put on her shoes properly. Maybe the tightness of her twists was making her paranoid. As she continued on out of the building she shook her head at a woman cupping her phone protectively as she conversed frantically on the phone. If the woman's intention were to not have the phone spotted by the youths, her twitchy demeanour alone would make her a target for robbery. It did not help that she possessed rather large incisors that resembled those of a squirrel. Bless her! Lolu figured she was probably new to the area.

Lolu delighted as she arrived at Marley's Fried Chicken Shop. They couldn't serve her curry, but she was too famished to care for such specificities. Food was food.

As she chewed heartily on a BBQ coated chicken wing, she didn't hear the crackle of the police radio. A plump policeman and lean policewoman stood over her table, their eyes yo-yoing between each other.

"Miss Tanine, you are under arrest on suspicion of fraud and the murder of Victor Timothies. You do not have to say anything, but it may harm your defence if...."

Lolu looked up and wrinkled her forehead. Were they talking to her?

"Don't make this harder than it needs to be, Miss Tanine."

"What?" The wrinkle in Lolu's forehead deepened. "That's not my name. You've got the wrong person." She tried to sidestep the two but the female officer grabbed her.

"Let go of me!" Lolu writhed about knocking the hat off the policewoman's sleek blonde bun.

"Stop resisting." Still, Lolu thrashed like a baited fish. "Fine. We'll do it your way." The male officer clamped a set of cuffs onto Lolu's hands.

"Let me go." Lolu shook her wrists. "I'm innocent. I didn't do anything."

Neither officer yielded. Those that they arrested always claimed they didn't do anything, only for the evidence to say otherwise.

Enticed by the sight of the next social justice story, a grey-locked man planted himself between Lolu's table and its three subjects as he brazenly recorded the situation on his phone.

"Get back!" The male officer said tersely.

"Don't take that tone with me," the man retorted. "I'm twice your age."

"Yes! Tell him, brethren," affirmed a woman draped in a shawl. "He can't talk to you like that!"

In an instant, a fleet of people docked at the shop's entrance eager to gobble up the scraps of spectacle. Some recorded stealthily on their phones. Others contorted themselves to get the best angles for social media. Some were content to observe the drama bubble up in the cauldron. Others heckled the officers whilst goading Lolu to break free. Lolu just wished that the crowd would shut up and move. Their flapping eyelids and flashing cameras unsettled her, and she could tell they were having the same effect on the police officers by the increased pugnacity with which they held her. They didn't need to hold so tight; she had resigned from resistance. The policewoman muttered curses upon the crowd subjecting Lolu to her coffee emanating breath, whilst her capacious counterpart beckoned at the crowd to disperse to little avail.

It was a relief then to see whirring blue lights and hear the howl of a compact police vehicle. The first officer to exit the car was similarly compacted. There was no room on his face for smiles, his biceps protruded from underneath his uniform and by his presence alone he herded the people to one side. His companion, a freckled officer bore a diminutive stature compared to his three colleagues, yet his humble authority was clearly acknowledged by them. The initial male officer stammered the details of the situation to his fellow colleagues whilst gesturing about the car, Lolu and the female officer, much to the latter's irritation.

Lolu was too tired to not comply with instruction so she allowed herself to be guided into the cramped backseat. As the muscular officer closed the door behind her, a twist jammed in the door. One thing was certain; a bald person would not have found themselves in such a predicament.

I feel that everyone should have a story that relates to them or helps them to relate to others because representation and empathy are so important. And since the vast majority of us have hair, who cannot relate to getting an unfavourable hairstyle!

- Jasmine Omogbehin

Published by Casey Elisha
(c) 2020 Casey Elisha
All Rights Reserved
For all enquiries, please email
CElishaBooks@gmail.com

ISBN: 978-0-9935264-6-6

Printed in Great Britain
by Amazon